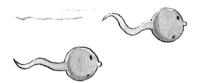

This book belongs to

WITHDRAWN

· ·

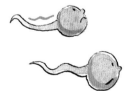

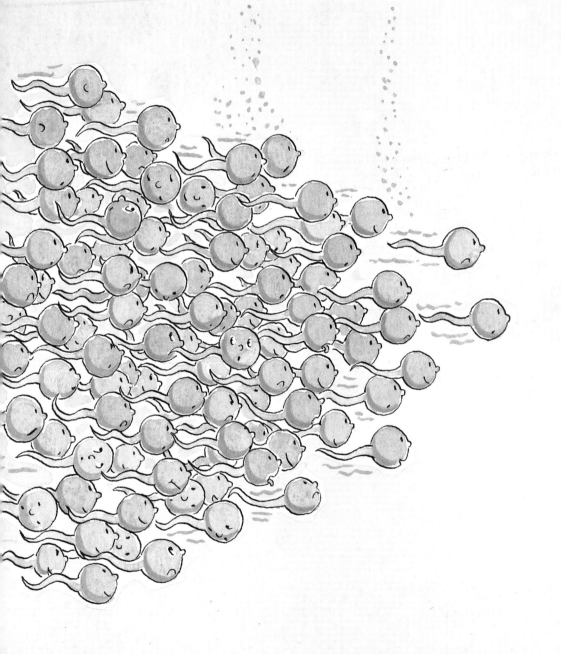

Where Willy Went . . .

Nicholas Allan

RED FOX

Willy was a little sperm.

He lived inside Mr Browne ...

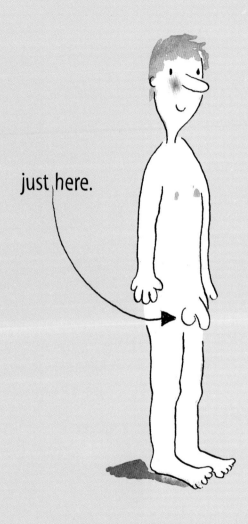

just here.

He lived with 300 million other sperm and they
all lived in Mr Browne at the same address.

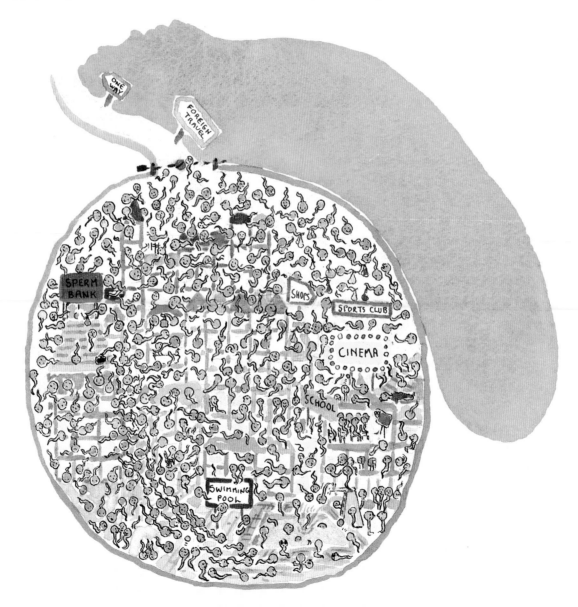

At school, Willy wasn't
very good at sums.

But he was VERY good
at swimming.

So was Butch.

Soon it would be time for the Great Swimming Race.

Willy practised every day ...

LIFT

and so did Butch.

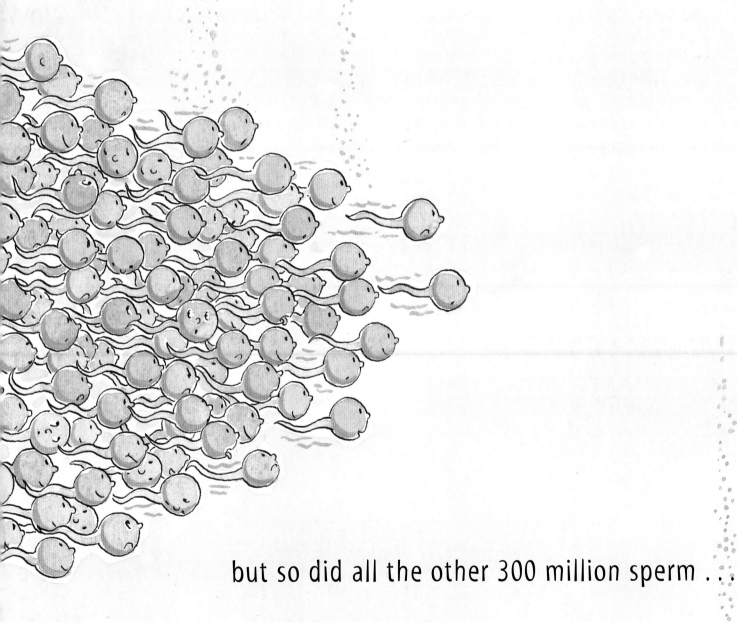

but so did all the other 300 million sperm . . .

But there was only one prize – a beautiful egg.
The egg was inside Mrs Browne . . .

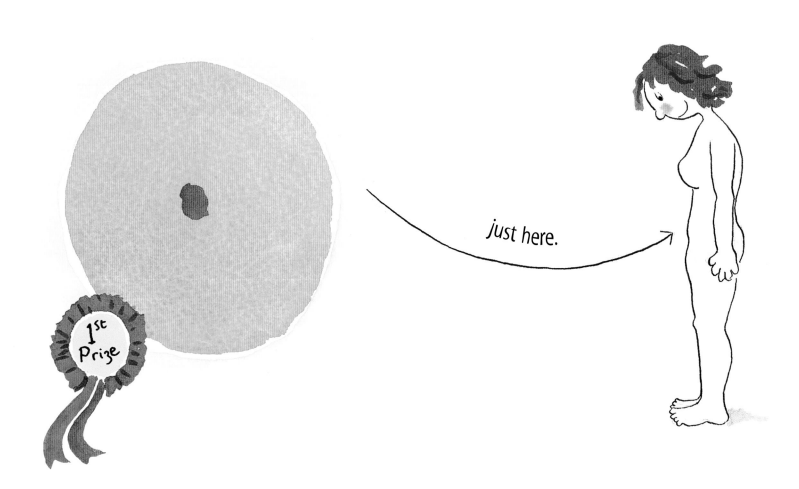

just here.

"If there are 300 million sperm in the race,
how many will you have to beat to win the egg?"
the teacher asked.

"Ten?" said Willy.
He wasn't very good at sums, but he was VERY good at swimming.

At last the day of the Great Swimming Race arrived.
The teacher gave them all a pair of goggles.

And a number.

And two maps.

The first map showed
inside Mr Browne.

The second map showed
inside Mrs Browne.

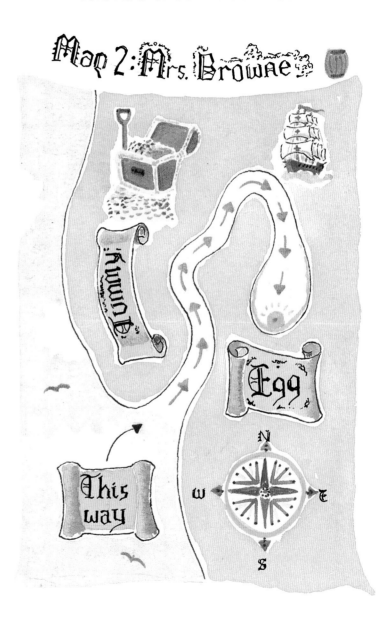

That very night Mr and Mrs Browne joined together.
The teacher cried, "Go!" and the Great Swimming Race began.

Willy swam and swam with all his strength. But so did Butch.

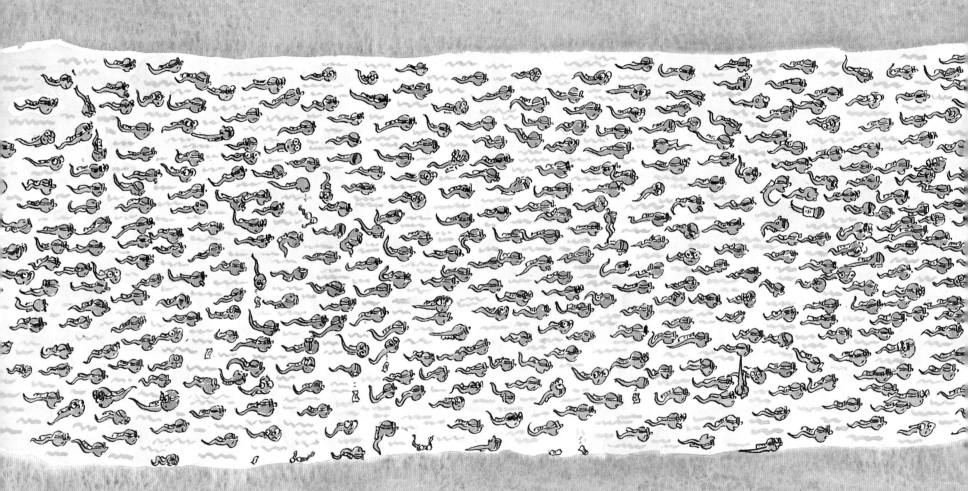

Butch was catching up. How much further did Willy have to go?

Willy swam as if his life depended on it. Yet so did Butch.

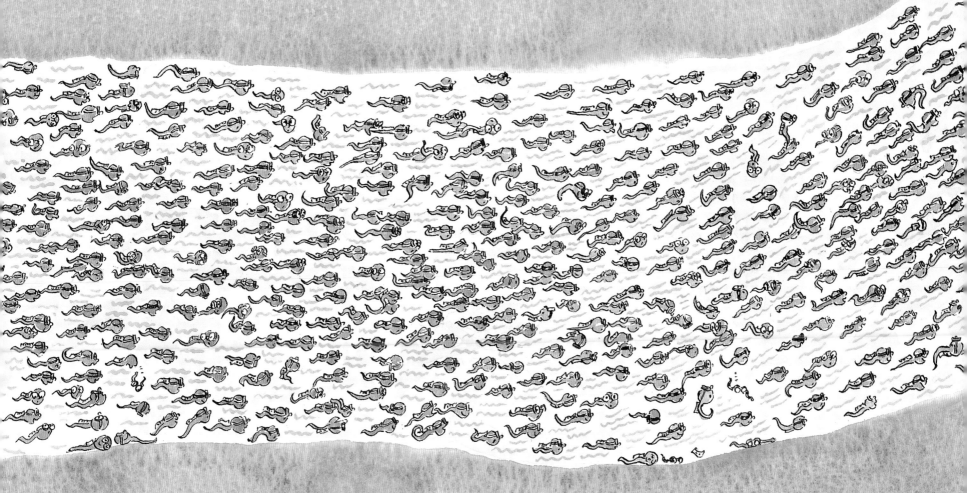

He didn't know. He wasn't very good at sums . . .

... but he was the BEST at swimming! HURRAH!

FINISH

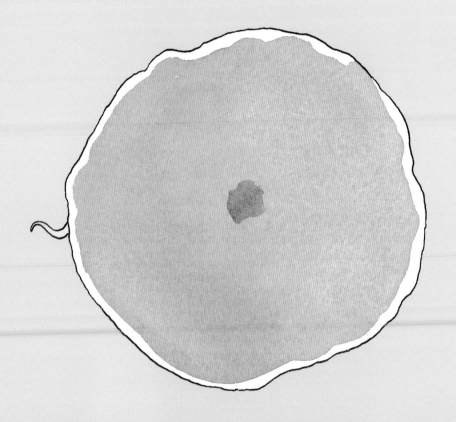

The egg was lovely and soft.
  Willy burrowed all the way in . . .

                        until he disappeared.

Then something
strange happened.

Something wonderful.

Something magical.

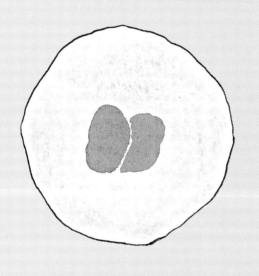 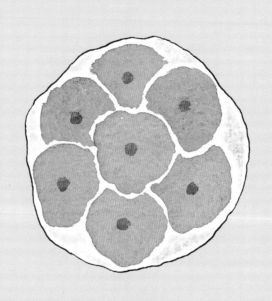 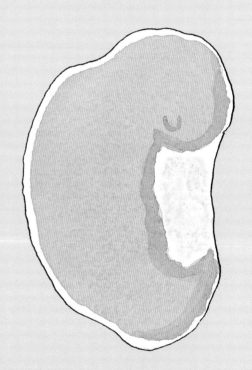

It grew and it grew until it grew bigger than the egg.

Something inside began to grow.

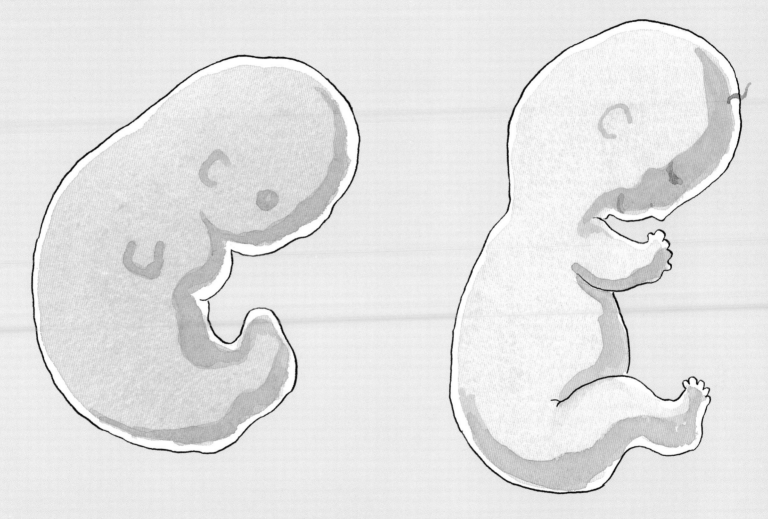

Then it grew some more until it grew bigger than Mrs Browne's tummy.

So Mrs Browne's tummy grew **bigger** instead.

It grew and it grew and it grew until . . .

the baby was born.

It was a little girl. They called her Edna.

But where had little Willy gone? Who knows?

But when Edna grew into a little girl and went to school . . .

she found she wasn't very good at sums . . .

...but she was VERY good at swimming!

The End

To Rod Stewart

WHERE WILLY WENT
A RED FOX BOOK 978 0 099 45648 3 (from January 2007)
0 099 45648 6

First published in Great Britain by Hutchinson,
an imprint of Random House Children's Books

Hutchinson edition published 2004
Red Fox edition published 2006

1 3 5 7 9 10 8 6 4 2

Red Fox Books are published by Random House Children's Books,
61–63 Uxbridge Road, London W5 5SA,
a division of The Random House Group Ltd,
in Australia by Random House Australia (Pty) Ltd,
20 Alfred Street, Milsons Point, Sydney, NSW 2061, Australia,
in New Zealand by Random House New Zealand Ltd,
18 Poland Road, Glenfield, Auckland 10, New Zealand,
and in South Africa by Random House (Pty) Ltd,
Isle of Houghton, Corner Boundary Road & Carse O'Gowrie,
Houghton 2198, South Africa

THE RANDOM HOUSE GROUP Limited Reg. No. 954009
www.kidsatrandomhouse.co.uk
www.nicholasallan.co.uk

A CIP catalogue record for this book is available from the British Library.

Printed in Malaysia

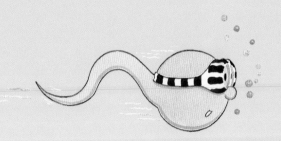

More books by the brilliant Nicholas Allan . . .

More and More Rabbits

Heaven

The Dove

Cinderella's Bum

The Queen's Knickers

Jesus' Christmas Party

Jesus' Day Off

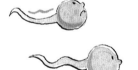